I0624927

THE LEGEND OF KALAJ

The Second Story in the Skaluni Series

BRUCE E. ARRINGTON

Copyright © 2024 Bruce E. Arrington.
Published by Pipe Dream Books.
Cover Art By Dilan Pramoda
All Rights Reserved.

Print ISBN-13: 978-1-942031-32-1

Part I

I am old, and tired of my life. These cold whisps of wind blowing my gray hair around remind me of how a tangled mess it has become. Not that I bother anymore. When my husband Junera was alive, I did care. And even more recently, when my Skaluni was here, but not anymore.

I sit apart from the others of my clan: the young, the old, those so-called "warriors", the women, and those who don't fit into any category. I am ashamed of them all. My grief, and more significantly—my anger, makes me want to never associate with those who squat a stone's throw away. I want to move far from those I once considered my peers, my friends. Their blunders caused the death of my precious boy. I cannot forgive them. Not ever.

I turn my gaze out over this wondrous floating land of grassy prairie. I should still be amazed by it all, but only despair fills me. Skaluni was supposed to come with us. He saved us from the fires and destruction of our home world. He fashioned this floating landmass so we could escape and find a new life on Ayash.

Once we reach Ayash—that great moon we revere, I will live the rest of my miserable life alone. Perhaps the Howlers will visit from time to time, but the others, the villagers, I can do without.

I sigh as a young boy, only a season younger than Skaluni, walks up, smiles, and sits next to me. His warm hand takes mine, and I imagine I must feel chilly on his skin. His name is Raver and he is the youngest member of his family. He's always been frail, thin, and pale. His bopa often remarked how Raver could not follow in the family tradition of hunting unless he grows more *jool*.

I don't know how anyone can force something like that on a child. Rismor wants his son to be like him, and that I understand, but Raver wants to be himself, and he shows that in subtle ways. His hair covers his eyes, and I remember a few conversations I overheard Raver and his bopa had over that.

Raver stares at the ground as his sister, Nyser, walks up to me. Unlike her brother, she's tall for her age, with long and smooth hair. She is a year older than Skaluni. She kneels beside me and embraces me before taking my other hand. These children are quite warm! I feel my heart melt. Perhaps I am being too hard on the others. Not everyone played a part in my child's death. Certainly not these two.

We don't speak, as there doesn't seem to be anything worth saying. But tears form in Raver's eyes and flow down his face. Nyser looks at him and does the same. The water lands on the soft grasses around us and I find myself joining in their sorrow. It comforts me to know they will miss my boy.

Our small band of three increases by several young mothers and their squirming children. As is tradition, we form a circle, sitting and clasping each other's hands. The bowed heads and bodies express the grief they share with me. It moves me, making me wonder if I misjudged them. Did they care about Skaluni after all? Was their grief the same as mine?

But a man's harsh voice interrupts our grieving.

"Raver! Nyser!" he calls. That warrior. I consider him a mere hunter, since all the men do is hunt these days. Dyalocal likes calling them warriors as if they are grand and important. But we haven't fought an actual war for years.

The hunter who calls to his children is one of several who loosed an arrow that killed my son. I cannot bear to look at him.

Raver and Nyser stand and glance at me, their red eyes still leaking tears.

Raver's shoulders droop as he leans in, whispering. "Skaluni was my friend. I will miss him."

"Thank you, Raver," I reply, my voice breaking. "He liked you too."

Nyser nods as she turns and walks away.

Soon the others leave until I sit alone once more, and my grief envelops me again. Only a few hours ago, my world was consumed by a great orange fire. Skaluni, my beautiful, wonderful adopted boy, died, caught in a crossfire between the hunters and the Howlers. After being struck with long, ugly arrows, his life bled out in minutes.

The Howlers had moved to the other end of the island, away from the hunters. Yet I know the hunters will go after them, and Skaluni's sacrifice will be for naught.

I blame Dyalocal, the tribal elder, most of all. He encouraged everyone to mistreat the boy ever since he was soho. And why? Because Skaluni's father, Cajus, a distinguished hunter of the tribe, died of a mysterious illness on the day he was born. And his mother, Verves, passed into the next life six years later. That was supposed to be the boy's fault?

Ridiculous.

But there was something else. Something obvious to any newcomer who would have shared a meal with the tribe. Skaluni didn't look like any of them. His hair was golden as the sun when he was happy, but by some miracle could change to red like fire when he felt angry, or white as snow when he was afraid. His eyes often reflected the richness of clear skies, and his skin the color of light clay that was found in the hills and valleys. But yet even his eyes and skin often varied in their hues. No one in recent memory had ever looked like he did, nor could they change their appearance as often as he seemed to; most of them had hair and eyes dark as night, and skin the tones of the Ilim they hunted for fur and food.

That was why they rejected him. Superstition and fear ruled all, as it ever had. Even my husband, Junera, who led the tribe for more than twenty years, would have looked upon the child with suspicion. But he was also a good man and would have stood up for this poor, innocent, beautiful child. At least, I would like to think so.

Tears flow freely as my body shakes. Sorrow drowns me, clouding my happiest memories of my past. Life is so cruel, so unfair, and I am utterly alone. I miss being his momo, and the pain from that loss is beyond bearable.

I take a full, deep breath, and another. I stare at these hands that will never hold my beloved Skaluni again. The skin is wrinkled, spotted in places, and can't bear the cold like it used to. But my hands were an extension of my love for this boy I embraced so many times! I close my eyes, remembering when I tickled him and he would laugh until his skin, hair, and eyes changed to those happy colors! It made me feel important, and worthwhile.

I open my eyes and look at the tall green grass in front of me. The stems, topped with small purple flowers, trigger happy memories. Once, in our home world, Skaluni and I walked together across a long plain, filled with flowers just like these. I never stopped to smell them because my back and legs hurt, and bending over was more work and pain than I cared to experience. But Skaluni rolled around in the grasses, laughing and pretending he was an aughi. He even learned to bark like them until I thought his mimicking was uncanny.

I pluck a stem of the grass and bring it to the tip of my nose. I hesitate before inhaling deeply. I always assumed these purple flowers would give off an attractive fragrance. Yet it is anything but that, and I find myself choking on the smell of burnt wood.

Is this the same flower? How was it that Skaluni was as happy to bring these grasses to his face as he was with the sweet-smelling blooms that grew around the Forsaken Hut?

"Momo!"

I can hear his voice. It haunts my soul as it echoes in my mind.

"Momo! Come out and play!"

The sun's warmth comes and goes, and I drift in and out of sleep. I can feel the floating island pitch in slightly different directions from time to time. When the wind turns cold, I find myself not caring. I don't want to move, or talk, or eat. I simply want to remember my child's last words repeated in my mind: a message to remember forever.

"I believe," he had said. "Tell Dyalocal the Moon Spirits made me for a purpose. I will join them on Ayash and tell them you are coming. You...and the Howlers. Promise me? Please?"

The emotions of those terrible moments hit me with full force. I had knelt by his bleeding side as he spoke to me, his life slipping away. It was so hard to focus, to concentrate on his intentions, with everything erupting in chaos.

I ponder his words. "I will join them on Ayash and tell them you are coming."

Was Skaluni only trying to make me feel better as he was dying? Or did he mean I would see him again?

That child never said anything he did not mean, which is another thing that set him apart from anyone else I have ever known. But did he plan to join with the spirits where they were traveling? Did that mean there is more than one spirit on Ayash? My people believe that each world or moon has one spirit that rules over it. Did Skaluni know something we do not?

I promised to convey Skaluni's message to Dyalocal, and I will, but only when I choose, and not before. Even thinking of that man makes me angry.

I refocus. The boy assured me he would join us on Ayash; those words I would have expected someone else to say to bring me comfort. But he cannot join us on Ayash. He is dead, killed by the arrows of hunters, who tried to ward off the Howlers, the same beasts that this wonderful child created.

I feel worse. I hate those hunters!

I stay put on the soft grass, glancing toward the other villagers on occasion. They cluster together like a pile of rocks. Only a few dare to wander off to fetch fuel for their ever-growing fire. It is quite bright, and I imagine I can feel its warmth. But my pride causes me to stay away, though Raver and Nyser call me from time to time.

The sky turns dark, and the moon Ayash is easy to see. The stars seem brighter too. At this rate, I wonder if it will take several days before we reach Ayash since it still seems so far away.

However, I suppose there is no rush as long as we have enough food and water to last the journey.

I assemble and organize the things I brought with me onto this floating landmass: some clothes, utensils, food, bedding, a tent, and a few toys Skaluni made for me when he was younger. I handle the toys carefully: a Howler, woven in long thick grasses, dead and brown; a fish made of clay we heated in a kiln we constructed, and a picture of us he drew on the skin of an Ilim. The image shows me holding his hand. Emotions sweep over me again and my pain reignites.

Weariness overtakes me so I clear my mind and pitch my small tent. Before long, my bedding is in its proper place, and the food bags are arranged. The air turns cold so I make a small fire. I sift through a few pieces of dried meat in one food bag before I find one to my liking. The cold air bites at my fingers and my face, causing this old body to shiver.

After I swallow the last of my meat, I'm more tired than ever. I barely have enough energy to put out my dying fire and crawl into bed. As soon as I lay down, I black out.

But at some point, I stir and open my eyes. It must be the dead of night, and it is so cold. So bitterly cold. What woke me? I listen and hear a voice. There it is again. Someone is calling to me, someone I know and love and so wish to see.

"Mo-mo!" comes the ghostly sound. "Mo-mo!"

I sit up, grab a blanket, and wrap it around my cold shoulders. As I step out of the tent, I listen for that sound to come again. But now, everything is different; I am not on Skaluni's island anymore. In this place it is day, and bright light shines on a new terrain. Ridges and hills rise before me, high and lofty. I see a forested region, a large lake, a desert, and caves. My eyes take in everything as I search for any sign of the sweet voice.

Something or someone stands off to my left. It looks like a person, and yet not a person. It reminds me of a silhouette as it shimmers in dark blue, red, and white. It raises an arm, pointing at large caverns on its right. Black and gray rocks dot the landscape around the caves.

What does this all mean? Why is it pointing to a cave? Am I supposed to go there? Is that where Skaluni will be?

I take a single step toward the pointing figure. Suddenly there is a blur, and I am standing near the largest cave entrance and peering at its expansive ceiling. But there is little else I see but a hollowed-out hole, filled with darkness.

"Momo! Meet me here!" comes a faraway voice that sounds like my boy. "Bring the others!"

Why do the words sound like a distant echo?

Where is he?

An instant later, I stand outside my tent, staring at the cold blackness of night, the moon Ayash closer than ever. The wind bites at me as I blink repeatedly, my eyes scanning the stars. I shake my confused head and return to my rest.

But I am unable to sleep. What just happened? What did Skaluni mean by telling me to meet him at the caves? And bring the others? Did that mean the Howlers or the entire village? I doubt the leaders would find anything valuable in a cave, but more than that, I don't want them to come with me.

Or could this be only my imagination, stemming from a strong desire to see my child?

After Ayash moves below my view, I finally close my eyes.

*

I wake to find the day partly gone. Bright sunlight and warm air fill my tent. Something changed. I sit up, trying to clear my head, and I see the Howlers. They surround my tent, some sit upright, while others lay down. They look menacing with their huge bodies and coarse, dark fur, but a few of them whine as if worried.

I roll out of my bedding and step out of my tent to find the entire clan watching me: hunters, elders, men, women, and children, all staring in my direction. Since when does an old woman forfeit her right to privacy?

Some of the hunters ready their bows and arrows. Are they going to shoot the Howlers? Anger takes over. I point at the hunters and shout.

"Away with you! Leave us in peace!"

The villagers look at one another with doubtful faces. Some shake their heads at me while talking to one another. Not a single one of them moves except the elder leader, Dyalocal. He lumbers toward me as his eyes scan each Howler. Finally, he looks at me and attempts a disarming smile.

"It appears we have arrived on Ayash," he says in his low voice. He motions to the crowd behind him. "We await instructions."

I realize Dyalocal doesn't have a clue as to what his next move should be. If we are on Ayash, he is out of his element, though he would never admit it. And if he makes the wrong choice, he gets the blame. So he turns to me so I can agree with whatever he wants.

I have played this game many times.

"Instructions?" I demand. "For what? Why are you asking me?"

His smile is so recognizable. He's trying to humor me. Probably because I am supposed to give my opinion before he does what he wants.

I am not going to play this game.

"What instructions did Skaluni give you?" he presses. "Are we on our own, or did he have a plan?"

There's the smirk again. It enrages me but I choose to stay calm.

"He probably did have a plan," I reply. "But your hunters killed him before he could tell me anything."

The elder's smile is gone. Perspiration runs down his face.

"I imagine he thought he would have accompanied us on our journey," I add. "It appears you are on your own."

The man lowers his head. "Yes," he admits, a look of sorrow appearing on his face. "His death was unfortunate. But did he not tell you anything that can help us?"

I am reminded of my strange dream. Go to the caverns. That's what the voice said.

I look at the landscape beyond. Forested hills are in one direction, a lake in the other, the desert in another, and finally, the caves, just as my dream had foretold. There can be no doubt—they are the same ones I saw last night, surrounded by those large rocks.

Why did the voice want me to take them there? Is Skaluni going to speak to them, or lead them where they can build a new village? Does he plan to care for these ungrateful, vengeful souls?

I remember a question Skaluni often asked me: Is it a good thing to wish the villagers well?

I used to tell him it was, never thinking about if they deserved it. I hoped it would help the people see the great good in my boy.

But they never did.

If I was to answer him, I would say no. It is better to leave them to themselves, let them go their way, and see how they manage. Even the children will grow to be like their parents: afraid and filled with superstition. I have seen it so many times.

It probably is better that Skaluni is not around because he would be disappointed in my response. Yet I no longer care.

I look at the tired and weathered face of Dyalocal. "Go where you must," I say. "But I will not join you." I shake my head. "The Howlers and I will live elsewhere, in peace. I will not trouble you anymore."

Dyalocal narrows his eyes at me as if I am a student who gave the wrong answer. "You are a member of our tribe," he says. "One with responsibilities to your clan."

I laugh. "I used to have responsibilities," I counter. "I raised an unwanted child for six years. Since you took even that away from me, I owe you nothing."

Dyalocal motions to those standing behind him. "And what of those children? Of Raver and Nyser? Or Drakim, and even your friend Denech? Would you part from them as well?" He gives a familiar sigh as his eyes shift from side to side. "We still value your counsel."

"And what of them?" I point at the Howlers, the giant dark creatures that everyone hates and fears, except me. "As soon as I join you, the hunters will have their way."

I am done with this conversation. I walk up to the nearest shaggy, black creature, and wrap my arms around it as far as they can reach. The beast just stands there, whining softly. Do I hear two heartbeats?

"We may need them for our protection," Dyalocal admits. "We do not know what awaits us here on Ayash. There could be enemies far worse than they."

"So you would keep them captive as long as they served your purposes," I reply. "As soon as their usefulness was gone, they would be, what?"

The elder smiles and laughs. "Only too well do you know our people."

"I will not come with you," I repeat. "Go. Leave me in peace."

For a few moments, the old man glares at me, though I pretend not to notice. Then he does something I don't expect. Dyalocal walks up to the same Howler that I hug. He reaches up and strokes its dark, shaggy body. His hand suddenly disappears into the coarse dark, fur and retrieves a knife, hanging by a tied string.

I remember that knife. It was the one Dyalocal gave to Skaluni on that fateful day he turned 12. As my boy lay dying he hung it around the Howler's neck. A wave of sadness sweeps over me once again.

"I am sorry for your loss," the elder says to the creature, looking into its eyes. "My people are afraid of what they do not understand, and there are many things we do not understand. We react instead of think and it has helped us at times to survive. Yet it may well have brought about our undoing."

Dyalocal returns the knife inside the creature's fur, retreats several steps, and looks at me with concern. "I would hope that you could put away your hatred of us, and see the needs before you," he says. "We have an opportunity for a new life here, and we would welcome your presence. But time is short and we must decide where to go."

I pat and rub the neck of the great beast before turning back around.

"I know as much of this place as you do," I admit. "You should choose what seems right to you."

The elder looks at me, a frown masking his face.

"But what about you?" he asks. "It would be shameful if you were the first casualty, trying to live out here on your own."

I smile as if I don't care, and I don't. I look at the caves again, trying to remember everything the vision told me.

"I will be fine," I say. "The Howlers will protect me."

"But where will you go? How will you live?"

"I think I will do some…exploring," I say. "Over there will be a good start."

Dyalocal looks where I am pointing before he laughs and snorts.

"You would live inside caves?" he cries. "Do they contain food? Or houses in which to dwell? Are they filled with enemies? Would you lead us to our slaughter?"

I smile, enjoying this discourse. He still thinks I want to lead them.

"Did you not hear me?" I reply. But he interrupts in a flurry of anger.

"Kalaj!" he shouts. "I saw you disappear last night. Moments later you reappeared." Dyalocal sets his jaw, which means he is finally serious.

I cannot hide it, so I do not try.

"So what if I did?" I ask. "What if I saw a vision telling me to take the people to the caves, not that I am willing to." Suddenly I catch myself and feel shame. Have I rejected my people?

"What are you not telling me?" the elder demands. "Is there something I should know? Did Skaluni tell you to go there?"

I shrug, feeling my shame disappear as quickly as it had arrived. "You must do as you wish, Dyalocal, as you always have. You brought us this far. I certainly won't stand in your way."

The man's face softens with a nod. "The people fear you will not come with us. Some say we should follow you."

It's my turn to snort. "Dyalocal, I am too tired to lead, and I have no desire but to spend my remaining days in peace. Let us leave it at that."

"I wonder what Junera would say to those words," he says, as he steps forward.

I turn to my long-legged friends and shake my head, and I realize I am at peace with my decision. It feels right. My husband would have agreed with me.

"As I have said, I will remain on my own, with the Howlers. They will protect me."

The large man sighs and gives me another sad smile. "I will speak to the hunters. As long as the Howlers do not come near the village, they might leave them alone." He turns his head sideways at me. "As long as you remain with us."

What is this new game he is playing? I hoped he would have been on his way, with all the other villagers. I don't want to live with anyone. But I look at the strong and large Howlers. All their eyes turn to me as if they are waiting for me to make an important decision. Must I trade my freedom for their lives?

I think of Skaluni, who would have done that in a heartbeat. So I turn to Dyalocal and nod.

"That is agreeable."

The elder hesitates. "I understand your hatred toward our tribe, but they still need you. Don't you still think it is good to wish us well?"

"No," I say, without thinking. "Not anymore." There, I said it, out in the open. Dyalocal can leave with a free conscience of never having to speak to me again.

But the elder's face shows no emotion as if he expected my response. After a few moments, he gazes at the far-away caves.

"What of this?" he asks, turning toward me. "You choose any five of our tribe. They will search out these caves, and see if there is anything of value. If so, that is where we will rebuild."

I hold my breath, not believing the words I hear. I don't remember Dyalocal ever offering a proposal so far from his self-interests. Is he truly afraid? Does he not have a plan for the people?

I sigh, realizing how close to being free from them I was. This elder leader gives me a counterproposal? And then I reconsider. Does Skaluni want us there? And if so, will he make an appearance?

"But if they do not find anything, would you agree to come with us, and with good intent?" the elder presses.

My first reaction is to say no. I doubt the hunters would give the caves more than a scarce glance. Perhaps they would not even reach them and say they did. But I have an idea, one which I know this leader will refuse.

"I will let Denech lead and choose the men. Then I will say yes."

The elder gives me a cold, calculating look, and I know I have him. He will never allow the men to be led by a woman, not even Denech, though she is worth any ten of them.

Dyalocal grunts and says, "She is a good choice. If anything is there that will help us, she will find it, and make certain everyone looks until there is nothing to discover."

"Then you agree?" I ask, hoping he won't. But I am not so sure from the look he gives me.

"I do," he says, with a smile. He turns and walks over to the other villagers. I hear his voice, though I cannot make out the words. After a few moments, several men raise their voices and I feel a sense of relief. The hunters will never agree to the Howlers living anywhere near them. I will be left to myself after all.

But there follows an even greater uproar from the women of the village. They shout down the responses of anyone trying to argue with them. And so by this, I know I lost my wager.

Part II

An hour later I watch as Denech, my long-time friend, readies herself with five hunters. She is half my age, with more energy than most of the men of the village. The hunters appear excited as they ready their weapons and provisions. But a look of fear escapes the youngest one, known as Tejib. He is not ready to be a hunter, even though he is 16 years old. Dyalocal often pampers him with false hopes of his future as a great hunter. Tejib often boasts, yet I can tell his heart is not in it. But for some reason, Denech picked him and the others, including Rismor, Raver's father. She has her reasons, of course, but he would have been my last choice.

Without ceremony, Denech's group passes through the tall grasses with their purple flowers. Soon they are out of sight. I look away to the caves in the distance, that seemed to have grown into small hills, many of their shadows falling to the north.

I sigh expectantly, though there is nothing to do but wait. But I'm not left to myself for even a few minutes, as Raver and Nyser return. After greeting me, Raver stares at the Howlers. Nyser sits beside me, but the frail boy remains frozen in place, his wide eyes staring at the dark, long-haired creatures. The nearest one gives Raver a short whine and the child jumps back a little, shaking all over. I smile watching his paling face.

"You are curious, I can tell," I say gently. "Have you ever met a Howler?"

Raver shakes his head. "Not close up. Skaluni asked me once, but my bopa and momo…" He hesitates, and his chin trembles. "They told me it would tear me apart and eat me."

I laugh so hard I fall over. "Nonsense!" I say once I regain control of myself. "Come," I add, offering Raver my hand. "You might not get another chance."

Fear covers the boy's features, and he hesitates.

"Will you trust an old woman?" I ask, trying my best to smile.

He looks into my eyes with a serious face. Finally, he nods, takes my hand, and helps me back to my feet. From there, I lead him to the nearest and blackest Howler. Its huge body lays flat on the ground. Its front paw is so large that Raver could easily hide beneath it.

I bring his quaking hand close to the Howler's snout. The creature lets out a sneeze, and Raver winces, but only briefly, and he does not back away. Within seconds a connection seems to form between this child and the Howler. Suddenly the boy's face changes from absolute terror to wonder. Raver kneels inches away from the huge animal and begins to gently stroke its fur with both hands. The Howler whines again, but this sounds more like contentment or pleasure. Raver laughs and smiles at me.

The boy stops massaging the long fur after a while and stares at this huge creature that so many speak ill of. During that short pause, the Howler props itself up, comes head to nose with the young child, and licks his face. The creature's tongue is overly large, and I grimace. But Raver wipes away the dripping saliva, laughs, and hugs the neck of the long-haired creature for a very long time. Sometimes he giggles, and other times, he speaks in quiet words I cannot make out. And from then on they are inseparable, as they chase each other in play, or roll in the long grasses.

A twinge of sadness hits me as I realize that sooner or later, Raver will follow in the footsteps of his father. All of this play will be forgotten as if it were an old dream. The child will grow to be a man of the village, full of superstition and fear like all the rest. Generation follows generation. Is there nothing, or no one, that can break this terrible curse of mistrust?

Tears spill over again, a mix of sadness and joy as I watch this newfound friendship. If only Skaluni was here to watch Raver and the Howler! I wonder how long it will last. My eyes shift to the villagers, still huddled together. I am curious to watch Lilor's reaction to her son's unusual attachment, but I don't see her anywhere. Is she not paying attention to her son's fate? Or is she not afraid of the Howlers like everyone else, but won't dare admit that because of what Rismor might say?

I wish I had gone with Denech and the others, so I could see what they see. I am convinced it was Skaluni I heard, telling me to bring the others to the caves. Did he make another wondrous thing? Perhaps another floating island, or other creatures, strong and trustworthy?

I would have slowed everyone if I had gone along, but then what would be the rush? Once we find what Skaluni wants to show us, I believe our futures will be bright and our fortunes will return.

I sigh and take in this fine, warm day. I lay back and enjoy the sun's heat, the island, and even the purple flowers. I watch as Nyser gathers a handful, along with their long, grassy stems. Her nose crinkles after she brings them to her face. Like me, she does not enjoy their bitter fragrance, and I laugh.

I wake to the sounds of loud chatter. The sun is almost beneath the horizon. As I look around, I find myself alone except for the Howlers. I must have slept for hours, and no one bothered to wake me. Where are Raver and Nyser?

Denech and her hunters are back. Excitement fills me as I hurry over to the clustered group of people, who eagerly listen to Dyalocal. The elder stops and waits for me to arrive.

"Since they found nothing, I suggest we turn our attention to the lake," he says in a placating tone. "We can catch fish and use trees to rebuild our homes." He looks around at the clan. "What do you say to this?"

Shock fills me as each member nods and murmurs in agreement. Nothing of value in the caves? How can that be? I remember my vision so clearly, and the words Skaluni spoke to me.

Momo! Meet me here! Bring the others!

Was I supposed to lead Denech and the hunters after all? Is that why he did not show himself? Or did I miss something in his message? It was real, wasn't it? Or was it all from my imagination? My strong desire to see him again?

The people stare at me as if waiting for a response. I look at Dyalocal, who also lingers.

"What?" I ask.

"What do you say, Kalaj? Should we continue to the lake, to find food and shelter for our people?" His face shows no emotion as I wrestle with mine.

I shake my head. "I am not your leader," I say. "But I promised to go with you, and I will."

I see the women's welcoming smiles. They nod as if everything has been reconciled and the disagreements forgotten. Several pat me on the back or place a quick arm around my shoulder and offer me food. Finally, Denech takes me by the arm and leads me apart from the others.

"No one blames you, Kalaj," she says. "Your suggestion to inspect the caves shows your concern for our clan. It comes with appreciation."

I stop and look at her. "I don't understand," I admit. "Everything in my vision was so real. I thought I heard his instructions perfectly!"

"I believe your story." Denech's eyes hold a guilty look, but just as quickly it changes to complacency as she nods at me. "When the time is right, we will go there together. I want you to show me what you saw."

Suddenly my confidence seems to evaporate. "I am just an old woman with no family. Perhaps it was my way of trying to reach out to…to…" My eyes water as I feel myself break down.

Denech envelops me in her embrace, holding me for a good while before letting go. "I never thought you a *draenth* for all the seasons we have been friends," she consoles. "If you say you saw him, then you did." She shrugs as if that is the end of it. "But my concern is for you," she adds. "I want you to be part of my family."

I shake my head. "You have enough trouble with your three children and that husband of yours." I snort and attempt a feeble laugh. "You don't need more."

Denech folds her arms. "Only Drakim remains with us. The others keep company with their friends, and we rarely see them. Ightosh will keep his opinions to himself and will welcome you. He would never allow you to fend for yourself." She looks around, checking to see if anyone is listening. "He misses talking with Junera."

"After all this time?" I ask, amazed at her confession. "He never said anything to me about it."

"He won't speak of it, but I see it in his eyes, especially after the council meetings. With Dyalocal, it has not been the same. Everything is different."

"As it should be," I retort. "Every leader brings different strengths."

"And weaknesses!" she says with a hiss. "I do not trust any of the council except Ightosh. I do not think they have your best in mind. That is why you must stay with us! Starting tonight!"

"But what of violating the sacredness of your blood family?" I ask. A longstanding tribal rule forbids us to live with those not related by blood.

Denech snorts. "I never accepted that terrible idea. If you had not taken Skaluni in, I would have. I told you that."

"Yes, you have. Many times." I am grateful for her words. "Though I am glad it was me."

Her face softens, her eyes water, and she looks at the ground. "I am glad it was you, too," she finally squeaks, and she envelops me in another hug.

"I will think about it," I finally say. "But I also consider the Howlers my family. I have to look out for them."

Denech fixes me with a stare. I can tell questions are running through her mind.

"Do you suppose Skaluni speaks through them?"

I wonder a moment at her question. Does she think the boy is alive? Did Dyalocal tell her about my dream? But I push aside that thought at once. Denech and Dyalocal have never been on speaking terms. And the current tribal leader only shares important things with his closest followers.

I shrug. "They are his creation," I reply. "And I'll not let anything happen to them."

*

As we stand together the next morning, the low fog around us disappears with the rising sun's warmth. Everyone carries their belongings except me. Drakim, the tall and muscular young man, insisted on taking my things with his. I look again at the Howlers behind us. Although Skaluni said they would follow me, I cannot justify it. They will be targets of the hunters or blamed if anything goes wrong. I will not let them die at my expense. But strangely, none of them look at me. Each is turned away, every one of them facing their massive heads toward the caves. What does this mean?

I know that going without the Howlers is probably a mistake. Without them, we have no protection apart from the hunters, whom I still do not trust. What if there are enemies far superior to the men of our clan? Who would protect us, then? But if even one of the Howlers was killed, I could never forgive myself.

As one, the men, women, and children move, still on the island my dear Skaluni created. It is quite large and it takes a while before we step off and onto the soil of Ayash. The difference is plain: only green and gray spikey shrubs grow here. Purplish pebbles litter the ground, filled with wide and abundant dirt paths.

The large, blue lake appears in the distance, surrounded by very tall trees with white bark and round, yellow leaves. I do not recall seeing them in our old world. The air is cool and calm, and the skies a deep blue, with only a few clouds near the horizon. Perhaps that is a good omen.

By mid-day, my legs are tired. Fortunately, the lake is near. The water looks deep in many places, and wide trees line it. I notice the leaves are not leaves at all, but round yellow lights, glowing bright or dull, spread throughout the branches. Green moss and lichens climb the trunks and stems, along with other plants boasting small white and purple flowers. I have never seen anything like them. Some trees reveal huge, thick roots plunging into the soil, or the lake water, roots so wide that any two of us could walk across them with ease.

Many birds sing from their branches. Their bodies are long, their tails are even longer, and their feathers flash with orange, green, and black.

This is a sacred place. We should not stay here long.

As we reach the cool shade beneath the nearest tree, everyone stops and looks around in a hushed silence. I take in the scene, awed at all the birds singing in the huge and wondrous trees. They look straight at us. Are they welcoming us? Are we supposed to greet them? Do they represent the spirit of Ayash?

Dyalocal clears his throat, his sounds a sharp contrast to the stillness around us. His large frame turns toward the people, his long arms outstretched. He smiles.

"Let us take our rest under this tree's protection," he says, proudly and confidently. "The hunters will scout for food and adequate shelter."

"Should we not pray to the Moon Spirit first?" asks a mother of three. Her long dark hair is set in braids, pulled back and her little ones dangle about her legs. She appears anxious as she looks from Dyalocal to the glowing tree above us. "For permission to stay? What if this place is blessed?" She frowns. "Or cursed?"

"Skaluni sent us here, so I doubt it is accursed," the elder replies with a mock grin. "Isn't that permission enough?" He eyes me but I turn away. I will not be drawn into his twisted reasoning.

Dyalocal has never shown much interest in spiritual things unless it suits him. That has always been my observation. Although Junera was never what I would consider superstitious, at least he respected the tribal beliefs and rituals. Dyalocal seems to consider himself above that.

"But you must do what seems fit to you," the elder continues, his expression placating. As we sit on the cool, moss-covered ground, the children run around the trees, chasing each other.

I feel irritated at Dyalocal's attitude but I am too tired to care too much. If he wants the spirits of this world to rain down on him, so much the better, as long as they leave me alone. And as for me, I lie down and take a rest.

*

Harsh noises wake me. Screams? What is happening?

"Rismor fell!" someone cries. "From the tree!"

I lurch up, trying to clear my mind. Lilor, Nyser, and Raver race toward the hunter, lying on the ground. Others rush to gather around him.

The tree above erupts with harsh cries. The birds of orange, green, and black squawk, fly back and forth and make threatening gestures with their wings. What made them upset?

"What happened?" I ask Denech, who stands by my side. "Has Rismor been attacked?"

"This is not good!" she says, her face scowling. "The hunters decided to shoot the birds for their meat!"

My eyes widen. "And they attacked?"

She nods. "In full force! Rismor killed one before the birds came at him."

"And Dyalocal approved this, I suppose."

"He told Rismor and the others!" Denech replies in a low voice. "The others retreated in time."

More shouting follows but from a different direction. The remaining men converge around Rismor and Dyalocal, gesturing toward the lake.

The birds in the tree above clamor until they fly into the blue skies. All at once they collide with each other, and change into dark clouds, expanding in form. What I see confirms my suspicions: this is a sacred place. We intruded.

"Stay here until I return!" Denech admonishes. "I won't be long." She runs to join the others, who cry in shrill voices.

Loud buzzing and clicking sounds come from the lake that demand my attention. I look to my left to see the strangest sight: beasts, the size of Howlers, emerge from the water. Dozens of them. Bright orange and yellow, they resemble oversized crustaceans I once encountered, many seasons ago when I was soho. Their narrow bodies and shell-like limbs enable them to move swiftly over land, and their tails have long, spiky projections. They race toward the confused members of my tribe.

My people.

"*I-ay-ee-oi!*" I shout above the noise of the crowd. I am startled at my volume.

Everyone turns to where I point, and several repeat the call to each other.

It is time to retreat.

Some make their way toward me, but others, like Raver and Nyser, remain next to the still body of Rismor. They do not move, and neither does he.

Several hunters take up positions to guard the mourners, and they wait for the water creatures to attack. I know there is no way they will defeat those monsters. I refuse to simply stand by and watch them get slaughtered, so I move to intercept. My legs still feel tired, but not as badly as before.

What will you do? A voice sounds inside my head. *You have no weapons.*

I hesitate briefly before my legs speed up. "I have to do something," I say, nearing where Raver and Nyser cry over their father. "I could not live with myself otherwise."

So you do believe it is good to wish the people well?

"At least those two!" I shout, tired of this conversation in my mind.

I see the dark, beady eyes of the enemy, closing in.

The entire clan stands together. Hunters hold their spears, or ready arrows, while the orange and yellow creatures race toward us.

A large shadow covers the ground and I look up to see clouds, dark and threatening, where just moments before there were none. The sound of thunder echoes above us. The leaves of the tree suddenly turn dark and refuse to shine.

It rains. Hard.

We have angered the spirits.

As Rismor is scooped away by one of the hunters, Dyalocal leads a slow retreat from beneath the giant tree. But I know it is too late. The monsters are closing in. They will overtake us and no spear or arrow will ward them off.

I am not surprised by the valor of the hunters, who are trained to save their people at a moment's notice. They form a barrier between the oncoming threat and their own: the women, children, and me. Some of the young men not yet of the hunter rank join them, eager to display their *jool*.

As for me? I become outraged. Angry with Dyalocal for being so foolish as to assume he can hunt and fish anywhere he chooses, and without asking permission from anyone, least of all, the spirits! I am also infuriated that my people are not able to protect themselves against an onslaught of this kind. My decision to leave without the Howlers was foolish.

Giant claws swing against the spear, and arrows spray at the crustaceans. Hunters dodge the fearsome creatures, and no weapons of our clan can penetrate the shells of these beasts. The rain drops harder, the light fails to a dim glow, and I am angrier than ever.

A few men fall, smacked away by the water monsters while trying to protect us. A madness overtakes me and, ignoring any common sense, I step in between the hunters and the crustaceans, waving my arms in all directions. I know this is the last thing I will ever do, but no other ideas come to my mind.

For a few breaths, all fighting slows and then ceases. I stumble on aching legs. My head hurts terribly. A weakness comes upon me and my vision dims to seeing only a redness surrounding my arms as they flail about. And then, most frightening of all, a voice roars through me. But it is not my voice at all. It is harsh, loud, defiant, and commanding.

"This tribe is under my protection!" I shout, yet it is not what I will to say, but something else that surges through me. My energy is almost gone and I stumble before Denech takes my arm and lifts me back up. But the voice continues, without willing to wait for me to catch my breath. "This hunter's life is forfeit for what he slew. So take him and be gone! Back to the water! Return to Oquau!"

The voice within stops, and my mind fills with questions. What happened to me, and what was that speaking out? What is Oquau, and why is Rismor to be given over to them? Is he payment for the bird he killed?

As my eyesight returns, I fall to my knees, awaiting a terrible death by these massive creatures. But the attack does not come. I look around, first to the men who stare at me in shock, their mouths twisted, their eyes angry. The water creatures wait, making more clicking noises with their tails and legs.

Dyalocal steps in front of the hunter who carries Rismor, and after a long hesitation, he leads the way toward the monster. Slowly the hunter kneels, lays Rismor on the ground, and backs away.

"No!" Raver shrieks. "Don't let them have my bopa!" He lunges toward the body but his mother pulls him back. Nyser stands beside her, helpless and weeping.

One of the water creatures scoops up the body in its long, thin arms, and backs away.

Shouts of rage erupt at the same time.

"Kalaj! What did you do?" a voice demands.

"Why have you given Rismor over to them?"

"They have not the right!"

"We would have fought to protect him!"

Repeatedly I am admonished, scorned, rebuked. Don't they know that wasn't my voice? How can I be to blame? As my strength slowly returns I rise to my feet. The mysterious creatures of the water vanish as quickly as they came. Denech shields me from the hunters who approach. No doubt they would harm me if they could.

Dyalocal raises his arms to the people until they settle down into a soft, sad moaning.

"We must permit this," he begins, as the rain pours over our heads. The wind picks up, bringing another storm with it. "For the present." He looks at everyone, from the angry hunter to the sobbing son and daughter, and finally to me. His face softens as his gaze returns to the people. "We cannot risk the entire clan for this, and Rismor would understand. We must locate shelter and protection. Let us move away, and find another tree to rest under. But do not touch the birds! Or the fish!" Dyalocal bows his head. "The Moon Spirits be praised!" his tired voice rings out.

"Forever and ever!" the people answer in a defeated tone.

"I think our welcome is past," Denech voices in my ear. "I doubt the spirits will allow us to stay."

"They will not," I agree as I look into the blackening sky. "As long as we remain, more of us will die."

As we approach another huge tree with round, yellow lights, I wonder if more birds are waiting for us. Will we be attacked as soon as we arrive? The sky is so dark that we can find our way only by this other tree's light.

Yet the wind increases, to the point of pushing some of the children onto their backs. The women scream as they gather their young ones. The rain turns to large chunks of hail, hard and cold. I look at Dyalocal, trying to usher the clan along with him. But I stay back, watching streaks of light coming from the dark sky. A thunder follows.

I will not join them. I turn and walk away, back toward Skaluni's island. Something tells me it will be safe there, and we won't be attacked by any more birds or monsters from the water. After taking several steps, I notice the hail lessens around me, and so does the rain. But Denech takes my elbow and I stop. I turn to see her soaked to the bone. Her son Drakim is at her side, shivering.

"Where are you going?" she calls through the wind.

"Back to the island," I reply. "You'll be smart to come with me."

Denech looks at her son, and then at the others, a confused mob of soaked, tired, and angry people. She nods and we walk together.

"We won't let you lose yourself!" she shouts.

Suddenly the wind calms. She laughs, looking at the clearing skies. "But perhaps it is we who cannot live without you. You are the only token of luck we have left." Under her breath, Denech adds, "It certainly won't come from Dyalocal."

My smile is weak, and I continue. The further we walk away from the trees, the brighter the night sky becomes. Soon the rain disappears, and the wind no longer blows. As warm air dries my clothes I feel hungry and after a while, I sit in the tall, lush grass. There aren't any purple flowers like those on Skaluni's island, but through the light of the other moons and stars, the grass leaves look the same.

I motion to Drakim who hands me my food bag, and we share some dried meat. After we rest a while, I hear the sounds of people talking and moving through the tall grasses. The *swish-swish* sound convinces me that maybe they are smart enough to know when they have lost.

One by one they collapse in the grass around us. Raver and Nyser still sob and won't look in my direction or even come close to me. Dyalocal, the last to arrive, stands and stares behind him for a long while before talking to anyone. As he walks by, I ask, "Did you lose someone back there?"

He stops, tilts his head toward me, and gives me a look.

"The hunters are brave and able. I have full confidence in them."

"To do what?" I ask, without thinking. Then I understand. "You sent them to recover Rismor?"

Dyalocal shakes his head. "They insisted. It was all I could do to convince most of them to return with us." A look of sadness crosses his face. "What next, Kalaj? Where is Skaluni when we need him?"

I don't know how to answer, though he doesn't wait for a response. He sits with the others, speaking to the women and children. But few will respond to him, and most turn away from his direction. They look defeated and worn out so soon in this new world! If I had any less self-control I would scold them for being so nicipi. But then I remember Raver and Nyser, and Rismor's body, lying beneath the giant tree.

I rise back on my feet, and without looking at anyone else, I continue my journey, ready to pitch my tent back on Skaluni's island and stay there. Denech and Drakim follow, and soon I can hear everyone else getting up and moving as well. "Let them," I think to myself. "But I won't be responsible for their lives. Dyalocal has to do that."

The clamor of the villagers grows louder as we continue our retreat. Through the darkness of night, they ask Dyalocal why we did not seek permission from the spirits before we went to their land. Why did he let them kill the sacred bird? Did he not know we were marked? Why was Rismor left behind?

 I can't make out most of what Dyalocal says in response, but I hear my name mentioned several times. I know they blame me for Rismor, but I do not care. I am not willing to put up with their confusion and superstitions any longer. I have to live my own life and not care about what they say or think of me.

As the sun begins to rise in the early morning sky, I can tell we finally reached Skaluni's island. It looks decidedly greener and more colorful with the yellow, red, and purple flowers spread out all over. Were there this many before? I don't remember.

Without bothering to pitch my tent, I collapse on the grassy ground and fall asleep. My last waking thoughts are about the Howlers. Will the hunters go after them because of me?

When I wake later that afternoon, I am lying inside my pitched tent, under a blanket. All of my possessions are here as well, thanks to Denech and Drakim. The air is warm and comfortable, and I roll over to see the blue sky. But the peaceful feeling doesn't last. I hear voices, and people talking in loud tones. Dyalocal's voice is among them, placating.

I sigh. Loudly. After yesterday's disaster, I am not willing to go out on any more adventures. Let them find a place and when they are settled come and tell me. Then I will decide if I want to join them, or not.

But when I try to stand, my legs hurt. I ignored the pain earlier when I was fleeing from the monsters, but now it feels like fire moving up and down, as if my muscles had been pulled and pushed too many times. As I slowly emerge from the tent, Dyalocal and some hunters see me, and approach.

"The memorial for Rismor and the others is set to begin," Dyalocal states in a serene tone. He looks at me as if waiting for some type of condolence.

But I am far from giving it. I stare at him, knowing that my face displays the true anger I feel inside. Dyalocal failed his people, blundering where he had no business going.

He tells me that five hunters perished trying to extract Rismor: Tejib, Berdar, Ukalo, Engias, and Smat. Most had a wife and one or two children, some even had grandchildren.

A large circle forms in the afternoon sun. We hold hands while sitting (painful as it is) and bowing low to the ground. The names of the hunters are repeated until Dyalocal stands to his feet and walks to the center of the circle.

"Oh Mighty Ayash," he begins, his voice expressing somber tones. "Today we remember those who have gone on before their time." I watch as he pauses. His eyes are closed as if considering. His hesitancy is unusual, as is his break in his speech. Finally, he utters a loud sigh. "First of all, we remember the boy, Skaluni, and thank you for bringing him to our village." I stare at him, wondering what he will say next, and am amazed at his words. "His great powers brought us here and saved every clan member from death in our old world. He chose to intervene to protect his creation when they were threatened by our hunters. He sacrificed himself, providing an example to always follow."

A few of the men murmur to each other—hunters, of course, who don't sound like they appreciate what Dyalocal is saying. But I do. His words are soothing, comforting me beyond what I expected to hear. My beloved boy is held high in memory. Water forms in my eyes and I wipe it away.

Dyalocal continues. "We also remember Rismor, who helped provide food for our village since he was soho. His skills surpassed us all, and he will be missed." He looks to Lislor, Nyser, and Raver and nods to them. I see tears streaming down the eyes of the children before I look away. I know they still blame me. "Smat would never back down against any enemy he faced," the elder continues. "His son, Berdar was like him, brave, true, fearless." Again, Dyalocal looks to the family members of those he mentions, and they nod back. "Tejib was like a son to me, and his loss weighs heavily on me and his family. Ukalo and Engias, the only twins for many moons, were the fastest racers this tribe has ever seen. May they all find their way to the hunting grounds of Nalwarendirtur. May you bless them with fortune and find their offering acceptable when they join you in the sacred realm of Cheverorm. The Moon Spirits be praised!"

"Forever and ever!" we all reply.

Five hunters lost. Everyone knew they couldn't beat the water monsters, so why did they leave us more vulnerable than ever?

Once everyone stands (Denech has to pull me up) we turn, ready to walk away, as is our custom. But Dyalocal lifts an arm, gaining our attention. "We will ask permission from the spirits to enter the forest over yonder," he says, pointing to his left. "If we receive a blessing, we will leave tomorrow."

I laugh to myself. Our leader asserts himself once again, not stopping to consider the consequences. Yes, he will say that he prayed to the Moon Spirits and received a blessing, but he has never offered any proof of their approval. When Junera was alive, he would sometimes wait for days before making a decision. Although I did not agree with every choice he made, at least I took comfort in knowing he carefully considered every alternative.

Denech looks over at me and shakes her head. I simply give a resigned smile and shrug.

"You agree with this?" she demands, walking with me to my tent.

"It does not matter if I agree or not," I say, slowly reclining onto my bedding. "I won't be going with them."

*

Dyalocal looks into my tent from the outside. He leans on his cane, his red face coming into view.

"You promised to go with us!" he states. "You cannot undo your vow."

I pull myself up on my elbows and look at him. "I did go with you, and you failed to deliver your oath of a new home to our people. You failed to ask the spirits for their permission to use their land, and we have suffered the loss of six tribal members." I feel my anger mount. "And you are doing it again by invading the forest? Have you lost your senses?"

"We were unprepared," he quickly answers. "Tomorrow we will bring the Howlers."

I nod in understanding and laugh. "As what, a sacrifice to the spirits?"

"I am serious," Dyalocal replies. "They will serve as our protectors. You can lead them. They will obey you, will they not?"

I tilt my head. "Skaluni told me they would, but I will not ask them to."

"Kalaj!" the elder roars at me. "We need their help! We lost six of our people. This has weakened us! Will you simply stand by and watch more of your people perish?"

"I would rather sit," I say. "Or lay down, as it best befits me. My legs will not work anymore today or tomorrow. I do not know when they will, so do not ask and test my patience further!"

The color drains from his face as he realizes what I say. Never in long memory have I admitted a weakness to him, and he has to process it.

"We can carry you, or you can ride on the back of a Howler," he says.

"You cannot spare people to lug me into that forest where more of you will certainly die," I say with a quiet sense of dread. "And I will not ask the Howlers to come with you."

Dyalocal's face turns into a scowl of contempt, and he turns away in a rush. I breathe a sigh of relief, glad that he is gone. I lay back down to rest but Denech enters and kneels at my side.

"He did not look amused," she says with a smile. "Here." She offers a hand. "Allow me to examine." She pulls me up into a sitting position and uncovers my left, swollen leg. After a moment Denech covers it back up and sighs. "It is tired and needs recovery time," she says, not looking at me. But there is something about her voice that I do not like.

"What?" I ask.

She smiles. "I was hoping Drakim might stay and care for you if you were wounded, but you are not."

I understand her meaning. "Is he excited to be a hunter?"

Her smile vanishes. "Yes, but I would rather he tend you in my absence. He would think it beneath his place if he had to nurse you."

I laugh. "He will be the best hunter of our tribe someday. You have seen to that."

Her gray eyes are piercing. "Dyalocal is sending him on a mission of no return, to the desert. It seems he is preparing for another defeat even before we leave for the forested lands."

"Ightosh is not going with him?" I ask, choking.

"Of course he is," she stammers. "But Drakim is the smarter of the two. My husband lacks sense at times, as you know."

I laugh. "But you have gotten him out of trouble before."

Denech shakes her head. "I am a leader of five hunters. We scout the forest tonight. I may not see either of them again."

I take her arm with my shaking hands. "Refuse!" I entreat her. "Say you will stay and help protect the mothers and young children who wish to remain here!"

"That will be your task," Denech says with resignation. "And to make sure the Howlers keep their distance."

I try one more time. "Make him listen to you! I know my vision is true! Skaluni wants us to join him at the caves!"

Denech nods. "I tried, but he will hear about it no more. His mind is made up."

"Then Dyalocal has condemned you all," I say with bitterness in my voice.

"I agree," she says with a nod. Her words turn quiet, slow. "That is why you must stay alive and safe. There will likely come a time when you will have to lead the people, or what is left of us, whether you desire that burden or not."

I gasp. "May it never come to that!"

"I pray it does not, but time will tell us." She stands and turns. "I must get ready."

"The blessing of Ayash be upon you and the others!" I choke. My eyes fill with water, and my heart is crammed with fear.

Denech makes a peace sign with her hands. "And to you as well." And then she is gone.

Part III

I lay in my tent, trying to stay warm. Attempting to sleep. A cough and sore throat keep me up late into the night, and when I do drift off, I see visions that make me afraid. Denech and the hunters make their way through the darkness of the woods, stumbling, sometimes tripping in holes they don't see. Denech tires and stops. Her face looks strained as she whispers to others. Then they move on.

It all seems so real. I feel I am with them, and I sense my legs twitch, trying to keep up with their movements. My muscles are sore and tired. That's when I wake for a short while before returning to a dark dream again.

Running. Screaming. Shouting. Are the trees moving? Nothing makes sense, everything is a blur. I can see hunters a little better in the growing light. They point at the trees, except that those are not real trees. They rest on the backs of odd creatures. One is a brown reptile with a long snout, sharp teeth, and an extended spiky tail.

Denech rushes toward one of the hunters who falls into a deep chasm with a scream. But it is too late. He is gone.

I wake panting and sweating in the late morning. Will Denech be hurt, or not return at all? Was this dream a sign of things happening, or simply what my fears produced? I wonder about Ightosh and Drakim, sent to wander around in the desert. Will they have luck finding us a new home, or will it be their end?

I take a few minutes to cough and clear my mind before hobbling out of my tent. Cold air greets me and I look into the cloudy sky. A light, chill breeze blows.

All the women, girls, and boys under 15 years old sit around a crackling fire. Some cook food with their sticks. Others simply try to stay warm. I look out to find the Howlers who circle our camp while keeping a respectful distance.

"Welcome, Elder Kalaj!" Vesran says, and she smiles. She holds a baby at her side. I remember when she gave birth to her firstborn, and it seems so long ago when I was with her during her labor. The tiny boy's head reminds me of the round melons I used to grow back in our old world.

Vesran hands me a piece of meat and I gratefully receive it. I sit next to her as my legs complain. As I glance around at the others, most of them look away. None appear confident or happy, and I understand why. This new world has brought death and calamity, in only a short time. How many days have we been here? Three? Four? And we still have no place to call home. Our food dwindles with each passing hour. The families are scattered and afraid, unsure of their futures.

Lilor, Raver, and Nyser huddle together eating their food and looking at anyone but me. I feel the sting return, and can't help but feel Rismor's death is my fault.

"When will they be back?" Vesran asks after I eat a few bites.

She means Dyalocal and the hunters he sent out.

I have no answers for them, especially when I think about what my dreams foretold. Most will likely never return. But they need reassurance that all will be well, that their husbands will be back. That they will find the food and shelter they seek, and that everything will be all right.

Every eye is on me as I give a confident smile. "Dyalocal divided the hunters into groups—some into the forests, others to the desert. It could be days before they return."

"Why would Dyalocal go to the desert?" Raver demands. "It is only wasteland!" His voice is sharp, critical. But at least he is talking to me.

I choose my words carefully as I look toward the barren, rocky grounds, filled with golden sand and occasional pillars of rock. They remind me of small mountain tops, smooth and worn, or like the teeth of an old person. "There is water on the other side of the desert," I explain. "Perhaps another lake, or an ocean."

Raver glares. "Won't the spirits send giant water monsters?"

I stare into this child's eyes. His face is stern, serious like Rismor's used to be. And there it is—he has turned into his father before his time. "They might," I admit. "Yet they could be merciful and give their blessing if we ask."

"What about the forest?" the boy persists. His eyes say it all: what monsters await the hunters?

My vivid dream, with the darkness and horrors, returns. But I dare not repeat it to anyone. That would drive them to despair.

"Denech will report what they find," I finally say.

Raver leaps up. "Tell the truth!" he demands, pointing at me. "You saw them, didn't you?" he screams, throwing his stick and food into the fire. He looks crazed, out of his head. "I saw them! Monsters carrying trees on their backs! They live in the ground until someone passes by. Then they come out, leaving huge pits to fall into!" He points at me. "This is your fault!"

Lilor takes Raver by the arm and slowly pulls him down. She massages his back and shoulders as the boy sobs.

"Why did you bring us here?" he asks. "Why is Skaluni killing us?"

Lilor pulls the boy in and embraces him. She looks at me.

"Elder Kalaj, please forgive my child. He is sick with grief after losing his bopa. We do not hold this against you."

Oh, but I know that is a lie. They all hold Rismor's death against me. I gave the command to turn his body over to our enemies, whether or not I consciously allowed it. But I will not let anyone desecrate Skaluni's name.

I stand with effort, my legs complaining again. I look at Raver, feeling my anger mount once more. But mixed with my annoyance is curiosity. How did he know of these monsters? How was he able to see them? Did he dream about them too?

I refocus.

"Skaluni saved us all," I say, with my best attempt at a controlled tone. "He did *not* tell us to invade the realms of the spirits, yet we did." I pause, looking at the women surrounding the fire. "He did *not* grant permission for us to go to the woods or the desert," I continue, my eyes searching the faces of the children. "That is what Dyalocal authorized. If you are to blame someone, let it be those who are deciding our fate today!"

I turn and walk to my tent, feeling the heat on my face. Shame fills me and I regret my harsh words. My task should be to bring comfort to the women and children, not cause them more anxiety.

Yet part of me does not care. I tire of the attitude of those who insist their way is right, that all others are wrong. What has that gotten us over the past generations? Infighting, lack of peace and safety, and insecurity. If it wasn't for these Howlers guarding us, I believe our island would have been invaded by now, overrun by those whose lands we trespassed.

An internal warning tells me that this is yet to come. That the monsters will soon grow bold and attack. Could the Howlers fend off an invasion if the hunters do not return in time?

That day I stay in my tent, trying to nurse my legs and rest. I drift in and out of sleep until Lilor calls my name. I welcome her in and she sits beside me. Her face looks serene, almost too calm.

"I am here to ask your kindness," she says with a grateful smile.

"Of course," I respond in like fashion. "How may I serve?"

"Raver and Nyser," she begins, her eyes looking only to the ground. Her voice is halting. "Both…love you."

I listen and nod but say nothing.

"My mind and heart fill with darkness," she continues. "I sense I will soon join my husband in Cheverorm."

My eyes widen, fear welling up.

"I am sorry," I say. A heaviness pushes against my chest. She is so young!

Lilor shakes her head but smiles. "My children will need help. I want it to be you. Be a part of my family."

"Me?" I choke out, feeling the responsibility wrapping itself around my neck, strangling me. "I am too weak to raise anyone's children."

"Look around and you will see very few of us left," she says serenely. "You care for the Howlers, and Raver found a new friend. I believe that is how he sees his visions. They are a part of him, and he sees what they see."

"Raver wants nothing to do with me." I know it is a weak argument. His feelings will pass. But I am desperate to be relieved of responsibilities at my age, not to add to them.

Lilor looks up at me, her eyes pleading. "Please consider?"

I nod.

Lilor bows before leaving the tent. "The blessing of Ayash rest with you."

"And you," I say curtly.

While I take another rest, a growing noise outside commands my attention. I ignore my aching legs and look to the skies until I see hundreds of birds, dark, with long tails, calling out in harsh voices. They remain a distance away, flying back and forth, not yet venturing on our island. They likely came from the lake, and I wonder if the hunters invaded their territory again. Behind them, the sky is dark with threatening clouds. Is a storm coming?

Everyone in our camp is on their feet, looking at the birds. The children begin to cry. I look around to see the Howlers, resting in a wide circle as usual, apparently unconcerned. I shrug.

"If the Howlers aren't alarmed, then I won't be," I say in a voice loud enough for all to hear. But the women still look fearful and agitated, and so I walk over to them, giving my best smile. "I think we will be all right since we are on the island."

"Please join us," Lilor offers, pointing to the circle where they all begin to sit. "We have some words to say." That is a formal way of telling me they all came to a decision of importance, and it is expected that I stay and listen without interrupting them.

If only I had remained in my tent.

*

The birds and dark clouds increase that afternoon, circling Skaluni's island. I often hear rumbling and other sounds, like an army is on the move. But by this time it is dark and no one can see much beyond where the Howlers lay, quiet and still. Doesn't anything bother them, I wonder? But finally, the noise ceases and we can eat our food in peace. By now there is only a little remaining. After this meal, we will survive on the few scraps we have left. At least there are small springs we can draw water from. For that part, Skaluni thought ahead.

What will tomorrow bring? I wonder if disaster will strike once the morning light returns. I have full confidence that the Howlers will chase away any who come against them tonight. But tomorrow, my heart tells me, will be different. We will be vastly outnumbered.

 My dark dreams return. Ightosh and Drakim run as fast as they can. Drakim is faster but goes back often to hurry his bopa along. A sandstorm chases them, slowing them down. It covers them before shifting and I can see them again. Suddenly tall giants appear out of nowhere, clad in rough skins and carrying spiked clubs. Father and son run away until they are lost in my sight. Finally, the winds cease, and all I see is sand, and then to my horror, a young hand sticking out of that sand, unmoving.

Even in my dreams, my heart is torn into pieces. Drakim was a promising lad, full of curiosity, hope, and the pride of Denech. He carried my belongings and never complained, though it must have been a difficult task. I scream and sit up in my bedding, shaking. And then I cry and cry, and cry.

Part IV

"Elder Kalaj! The Howlers! They are on the move!"

I wake to the sounds of screaming, crying, and howling. Everything outside the tent is cold and white. Fog is everywhere, and so is panic. Women run in circles, trying to find their wailing children. The boys shout at me, pointing in all directions.

So this is it. The end of my village, my people. And as for me? I don't care so much. I lived long enough and don't desire to stay one day longer in the land of the living. But poor Drakim. Nyser and Raver—what will become of them?

At least my legs feel better. It is a good start, I think. That way I will be able to fight. I square up my resolve and determine I will take as many of these cursed creatures to my death as I can.

"We will pack your things!" Lilor says, as she, Raver, and Nyser slip inside my tent and go to work.

The long-tailed birds circle above us. The women cringe and cry as they gather their belongings in a final attempt to leave this island that, up until this morning, gave us every protection we needed. But that is past. Behind me, the Howlers approach, and the enemy—the birds, the reptiles with trees on their backs, and the oversized orange crustaceans, or the *Sisaryg*, as we named them, follow closely behind. But ahead of me, I see our doom: giants, covered in fur and carrying long, spiked clubs.

I estimate there are hundreds of these creatures, all staring us down. I wonder when they will attack, and how many the Howlers can kill. As everyone else gathers around me, asking what to do, I find myself unable to answer. What do we do? We can't do anything. It's up to the Howlers to protect us now.

The darkest and blackest Howler walks up to me. The one Skaluni gave his knife to. Will it be the first to attack? But it doesn't look angry, or excited, or even frightened.

I throw up my hands. "What is wrong? Why are those creatures on the island? Why aren't you chasing them away?" My voice is shrill, nervous. But the Howler doesn't seem to notice my escalating fears. In desperation, I place my hand inside its fur and feel the warmth. It turns its black head and looks into my eyes.

Follow.

And with that, the Howler walks away.

That impression is too strong to ignore. But what does it mean? Am I to follow it to battle, to my death, to the deaths of these my people? Does it have a real plan, or will we surrender ourselves without a fight? A small part of me wonders if they are going to give us over. That they were against us all this time, and all they needed was the right opportunity. Without them, we are defenseless.

My feet lock in place and I do not move. Our lives are at grave risk, and I still have no idea what I should do. Why is this happening to me?

A small, warm hand slips into mine and I see Nyser, looking at me with a fierce determination in her eyes. "We will get through this!" she assures me. "Together."

My other hand is grasped by Raver but he pulls at me. "The Howler wants us to follow," he insists, looking at me with concern.

But for what purpose? My fears bite at me. I look at the boy, the one who hates me for forsaking his father. At least he is speaking to me now, so I allow him to lead.

As I walk forward, the rest of the fear-filled clan follows, everyone carrying their remaining possessions. The twelve Howlers close in, flanking our sides and back. The black Howler leads us forward, walking too fast for us. Many times it has to stop and wait for us to catch up.

My mind is blank and I do not understand what is happening. I look behind to see the birds and reptiles, gaining ground. They make little noise, but their very presence fills me with dread. Ahead, waiting in the stillness, are hundreds of giants, leaning against their terrible weapons.

Why we are doing this, I cannot imagine. If we are going to battle, why are we this close to the enemy? We could be wiped out in moments.

As we near the line of giants, the Howler stops and turns to me. I join it, confused as ever, stop and wait. In a few moments a large, black bird lands beside me. This long-winged creature is my size, with extended wings and an extensive tail. It turns its eyes to me and begins to squawk. And for some reason, I comprehend what it is saying.

I am the emissary of Caih. Can you understand my words?

"I can," I say. "But who is Caih?"

The bird tilts its head as if trying to believe what I just asked. It stretches out its wings and speaks again.

Caih is the guardian of the lake creatures. Are you the one called Kalaj, on whom the spirit of Ayash rests?

Spirit of Ayash? I don't know what this bird is going on about. But now is not the time to decide that.

"I am the only one with that name," I say.

I will speak with you, and you will retell my words to your people, the bird continues after a slight pause.

I don't appreciate the creature's bossy tone, but I check myself. Maybe they want a truce, to find ways we may co-exist.

"I understand," I reply with a nod.

When you hunted, Caih was displeased. Your people gave no warning of your intent to harm us, and so we acted in our defense.

I translate the meaning to the women, young men, and children standing around me. Their expressions hold mostly fear.

We understand you were seeking out food to feed your families, but a priest of Caih was taken. Priests are protected members of our race.

The people look at me with terror in their eyes after I translate, but I hold up my hand to them. I worry they may panic and run.

The man you call Rislor was not slain by us. He fell before we could reach him and prevent his death. Sending your other men to retrieve him was dishonorable.

Several women begin to cry after I translate. All hope vanishes from their faces.

If you had but asked for our help, we would have been pleased to guide you to Ayash. Yet even now, we do not consider you our enemies.

"You don't?" I choke, before interpreting the words to the others. "Does that mean you still mean to help us?"

We mean you no harm. To prove this, we are returning your family.

I do not need to translate those words. Out of a white mist walk five hunters, the very ones Dyalocal sent to retrieve Rislor. They greet everyone with tired smiles and hugs. One of the hunters calls Lilor and gestures to a stretcher that lies on the ground. A wrapped body rests on it.

"They have returned Rislor so we may send him on to Nalwarendirtur," he says solemnly, before turning to me. "Elder Kalaj," he continues, and he bows low. The other four hunters do the same, as Lilor, Nyser, and Raver rush to their fallen father's side.

I turn to the priest of Caih. "I do not understand," I say. "From the actions your people have taken, I concluded we are unwelcome in this world."

The large bird pauses a few moments before responding.

Not unwelcome. Ayash chose you.

"Ayash chose us?" I ask, amazed.

The bird flies away without another word, and my mind is filled with confusion. My dread is vanishing, but my thoughts are still disordered.

The black Howler leads us forward and the giants part to one side, opening a path. I realize where we are headed and I smile to myself. But once again the Howler stops, and we halt. Out of more mist arrives Denech, the hunters I saw in my dream, and many others from our clan. Some appear wounded, but otherwise, they seem all right. Denech looks exhausted but she greets me with a hug.

A grey reptile with a spiky back approaches and stops as the newly arrived hunters join their overjoyed families. It uses guttural syllables, yet I can understand its meaning.

I am the ambassador of Forgar, of the forest creatures. We found your family, lost and wandering in the woods. A few fell into our pits, but we brought them back, alive and safe.

I am beginning to sense that nothing is as it had seemed. These creatures are not our enemies. How could we have been so wrong?

"I thank you," I reply. "I will make certain that does not happen again."

That is wise. In the past there have been souls lost, ones we could not recover.

I make a bow to the reptile and it backs away, keeping its prickly spines behind it. And so we continue until the Howler reaches one of the giants.

I cover my mouth when, out of the mist, I see them walking side by side, safe. Ightosh and Drakim run to Denech and they hug and laugh and cry for a good while. My emotions get the better of me, and I can't seem to stop my flow of tears as the remaining hunters appear and unite with their loved ones.

I am Merol, says a giant rising in front of me. Merol stands head and shoulders taller than the others, and instead of wearing skins, he wears a long black robe. He also speaks our language so we can all understand. *I am the spirit and guardian of the desert dwellers. We are pleased that none of your family suffered grievous hurt during their wanderings. We stand ready to help those of Ayash, our friend.*

So much fear we felt. So much distrust we harbored. I am ashamed I was taken in by my prejudices, thinking I was above all of that. And here, standing in front of us, is an actual spirit, and not an ambassador! How did we earn that honor?

I bow to my knees in reverence and respect; everyone else in our clan does the same.

"We are honored by your welcome," I say with as much warmth as I can muster.

By now the mood of my people changes as we rise to our feet. There is laughter, many smiles, and heartfelt cheer from the men, women, and children. Even Raver and Nyser look at me kindly.

Merol speaks one last time.

There is one more of yours, Elder Kalaj, and he wishes to speak to you.

Everyone turns silent as, out of yet more mysterious mist, Dyalocal appears. He gestures and I walk forward until we are out of earshot. He smiles, looking dirty and tired. There is something in his eyes I cannot place. Joy? Peace?

"You have become united, I see," he says gently, looking proud. "The family of Kalaj."

I shake my head. "Their fears drove them to it. It means nothing."

His smile remains. "It means everything, and truthfully, I am glad. It is time."

"No!" I insist. "I will not lead them. That is your job."

He shakes his head. "I found a new path." He gestures at the giant. "With Merol." He breathes a long sigh. "The giants have many things to teach me. Did you know their bodies can appear in and out of a sandstorm?"

I am shocked and utterly unimpressed by his attempt at changing the subject. "You would leave your clan?"

"It is your clan now," he says in a quiet voice. "If I stay, the loyalties will remain divided. You know I speak the truth." He steps forward, offering his long staff, his rings, and his shawl. "These are yours."

"They are not," I declare. "Junera hated them and they will not touch me! I do not need signs or tokens of leadership. If people choose to follow, then they will. I do not need accessories!"

Dyalocal's expression changes as he lays the items on the ground and takes a step back. A heavy weight seems to lift from him as he continues. "Junera," he says. "I truly am sorry he is no longer among us. He was a great man, and a better leader than I."

What is Dyalocal doing? Why is he bringing this up?

"I thought you welcomed the leadership once he passed," I accuse.

"I did," he replies. "In the beginning. I was certain I could do better, but looking over these past fifteen years tells me that I was wrong. It should have passed to you."

I chuckle, not believing a word of it. "The leaders would never have accepted that."

"No, they would not, and that is another problem with our people." His face falls. "But when the opportunity came, I found perhaps a way to redeem myself and bring you joy after everything you suffered." His eyes shine, taking me by surprise. He looks away, wiping one eye.

I am in shock. "You knew I would take Skaluni? I thought you hated the child!"

Another tear falls down his cheek. He slowly shakes his head. "How could anyone hate that wonderful boy? He was more thoughtful, more kind than anyone I have ever met. I could have learned many things from him."

"But you kept him away from the village!" I cry. "You distanced the people by insisting we live in the Forsaken Hut!"

Dyalocal looks at me with a slight smile, allowing me time to consider my words. Finally, I choke, as I come to a realization. "Part of the plan, I suppose?"

"To give you a life you deserved, a child you could raise, away from the everyday judgments, scorn, and agitation that awaited you in the village." He sighs, looking at my large new family. "If only our world had lasted, I wanted to trust that all would have been well. That we would embrace Skaluni and put away our selfish traditions. Yet here as elsewhere, our beliefs and prejudices blind us to what is right in front of us."

"I hated you for that," I say, my eyes suddenly spilling tears. "And now...and now..."

"I know," he replies. "I accepted that hate if it meant you could find happiness."

"I did not know," I admit. "I am ashamed." Guilt sweeps over my soul and suddenly I feel very small.

"Of course, you did not know," he counters kindly. "To retain my standing as a leader, you could not be allowed to even suspect what I honestly wanted for you. Have you forgotten Junera's frustrations at our fears and superstitions?"

"He almost quit," I say, remembering the many sleepless nights my husband had suffered. "I often wished he would."

"I am grateful he did not relinquish his duties. And I hope you do not give up, now that our people are under one family name, which has not happened for many generations. That will make you a legend, in time." He smiles through more tears. "The legend of Kalaj."

I step forward and wrap my arms around him, and he responds in kind. Strong feelings for this man surge through me, emotions I had considered lost forever.

"Father would be proud of you," I say with deep emotion. "He always said you would turn into someone great someday. I never believed that until now!"

"Farewell, sister!" he says with a final hug. "The blessing of Ayash always be with you!"

*

After all the reunions, I feel my energy drain away. As our newfound friends return to their homes of lake, forest, and desert, I mount one of the Howlers. Not the black one, however. Raver took it before I had a chance to choose. But a gray and black Howler carries me with ease since my legs have given up again and I do not feel like walking. Denech rides behind me, claiming she is there so I don't fall off. But I think she is more tired than she shows.

The skies clear and the air turns warm as the caves come into view. They don't appear as gloomy and dark as I remember looking at them from the island. Most are no taller than me, grouped together in a mass of brown, coarse rock. But there is one that rises far above the rest and stands alone, black and gaping. I hear voices coming from its direction, drifting in the wind as if someone is calling from far away.

 This Howler makes the trip easy and fast. I look back, barely able to see most of our clan, walking toward us. Perhaps I need to offer some of them a ride, though I wonder how many would accept it.

"I have something to confess," Denech speaks in my ear, bringing me out of my thoughts. "Please do not be angry with me until you hear everything I have to say."

I laugh casually. "How can I be angry? You came back from the dead."

"Even so." She pauses, waiting to hear my reply. I do not like the sound of this. Are there more pressing problems for me to solve?

"All right, speak your words," I say.

"I found Skaluni when I went to the caves with the hunters," she says quickly. "But he would not let me tell anyone, not even you."

I turn and look at her, aghast. "Not even to me? Why?"

Denech shrugs. "I have thought about this as well and wondered. But now I believe the clan was not ready to follow him. They still did not trust Skaluni, even after he made that flying island that brought us here."

I sigh in agreement. "We were not ready, still divided in our minds and hearts. But does it require going to war before our people can unite?"

"Apparently," she says. "But Skaluni also gave me a glimpse of what there is on the other side of the caves," she adds with a laugh. "Everyone will be surprised."

"What did you see?" I ask eagerly.

But Denech doesn't say anymore, no matter how much I wheedle or cajole her. So I give up asking as we reach our destination. I manage to dismount, sliding off awkwardly at the end. Denech, however, glides off with ease, as if she rides Howlers every day.

It takes a couple of hours before the last of my people arrive. They look tired. The mothers are worn out, though most of the fathers carry the smaller children. We stand at the entrance of the largest cave, a gaping hole into the unknown. For a few minutes, we stand around and wait for something to happen.

And like magic, he appears. My boy, my Skaluni, steps out of the darkness. He is dressed in skins like us, but he looks different. Grown-up. Taller. His face reminds me of my child, yet how can he be so much older?

"Skaluni?" I ask in a whisper.

"Hello, Momo," he says, stretching out his arms to me. He gives me that wide smile I know so well.

In two steps I embrace him, shaking with joy and delight. His form is solid, so I know this is not a dream or vision. Yet so many questions rush into my mind I cannot contain them all.

"We will speak together, later," he says in my ear. His voice is soft and reassuring.

"I look forward to it," I reply with a smile.

I step back after releasing him, and join the others, who look at Skaluni with narrowed eyes, trying to understand, or rather believe, that this is indeed my boy.

"Welcome!" he says happily, apparently ignoring their stares. He points to the cave behind him. "I am here to bring you to a new home, where you'll not see any more destruction like that of your old world. There is plenty of food, and places to build your dwellings, live with your families, and be at peace."

"We are Kalaj!" says one of the hunters in a gruff voice. "Yet who are you?"

"I am glad you are now one family," this young man replies. "In your home world, I was known to you as Skaluni. But that body was destroyed by the rivers of heated rock. I returned here to welcome you to a new life if you choose it."

He looks to me for the answer.

"Of course we do!" I say boldly. "We've had enough conflict and strife. We need what you offer!" Perhaps being the leader of the tribe isn't such a bad thing after all, I think. I just made everyone's decision for them!

"Follow me," Skaluni invites, and as one we move forward, including all twelve Howlers, bringing up the rear. Once we reach a solid wall inside the cave, Skaluni simply touches it, and it vanishes. The people gasp in surprise, but what I see after this makes me cry out in wonder.

A raised waterway zig-zags across a backdrop of forested lands. Sheer cliffs run down each side of this fantastic river. Mountains rise on the left and right, and rock bridges emerge out of them. The bridges end where I see a large, flat pedestal. Beneath the pedestal is a support pillar reaching to the ground, far below. I count eight of these structures. Birds of different colors and sizes fly high in the sky above, as well as over the forests below. A white mist rises from many of the trees.

Flat and wide water vessels are docked nearby, ready and waiting.

"These will take you to Zekoyi, the main village," Skaluni tells us. "There the people will provide everything you need."

I turn to the clan. "All right, Family Kalaj! It is time to go!"

My family members are hesitant to follow. The waterway with its high cliffs seems to frighten even the bravest hunters. Yet the Howlers show no concern, as they each step onto a separate vessel. And soon the boats fill up. Apparently, Family Kalaj is convinced that if they are safe enough for a Howler, then they must be trustworthy. I watch the black Howler and Skaluni reunite. After my grown boy retrieves the knife around its neck, the Howler boards.

Skaluni helps me steady myself onto the flatboat. The Howler I rode earlier, along with Denech, her family, and others are already in place. We sit on low seats as a cool breeze picks up and the vessel is carried along by the current. I keep my eyes straight, not allowing them to peek into the abyss down at my left. I am not sure if my old heart could take it. Finally, I turn to Skaluni, who sits on my right.

"What is this place?" I ask, admiring the lush scenery.

His expression saddens me as he places an arm around my shoulders.

"Long ago other people lived here. I cared for them, and they prospered without any wars, diseases, or conflict, except for the troubles they caused for themselves. Yet they wanted more. Eventually, they chose to leave."

"They wanted to leave?" I say with a snort. "This paradise? That seems ridiculous. What did you do?"

"I let them go," he says in a voice barely above a whisper. "Sometimes I wonder if that was the right decision, but I will never hold any people against their will. I made an exit similar to the caves that brought you here and hoped that after a while they would return, but none ever did. After everything I gave them, it still wasn't enough." I place my hand on his as he gives a big sigh. "I was lonely without anyone to care for. Eventually, I knew what I had to do."

I think back to the miraculous signs that happened around the time of Skaluni's birth: the seven moons aligning, the land quakes, the mountain blowing itself apart, and the loss of water from our fish-filled lake.

"What did you have to do?" I ask.

"Find those who needed help, like your people." He shrugs. "I knew your world was doomed."

"Only us?"

He turns his head to one side and smiles. "No. Yours was the last tribe, as you'll soon see."

We sit in silence for a while, the wind and waves moving us forward. The day is beautiful and the air is warm. Billowing clouds rise in some places, and the sky is clear and azure in others. Suddenly the Howler in the back of our boat gives a loud and strange call. Then it disappears—right in front of my eyes! One minute it is right there, and the next, gone. Then I hear its call once more. My head turns and I see, high on a mountain bridge, the Howler settling onto the pedestal. Its body turns to stone and it moves no more.

I scan Skaluni's face. His eyes mist and I wish I knew what he was thinking.

"The Howlers helped us," I say. "They brought us great comfort when we were afraid."

My tall, strong, spirit-boy nods somberly. "That was their purpose."

I take his other hand in mine and turn him so we sit face to face.

"Do I call you Ayash, or Skaluni?" I ask.

He shrugs. "One name is as good as the other." A slight smile escapes his lips. "But you will always be my momo."

I laugh and look him in the eyes. "How can I tell for sure it is you?" I ask. "That you are that boy I raised for six years? You look so different. You are so different!"

His face brightens. "Do you think it is a good thing to wish your family well, to provide for them? To protect them from enemies, so they can live blessed lives?"

I think back to just days ago when my heart was filled with grief and bitterness at my great loss. I would have given anything to shun my clan and live alone for the remainder of my days. But now, it is not so. I suppose I am still able to change too. And hopefully, for the good.

"Yes," I say. "I do think it is."

Glossary

Aughi. A domesticated animal, similar to dogs but they can also be cat-like.

Ayash. The spirit and guardian of the human domain.

Bopa. The same as a father, though the term is generally used affectionately.

Caih. The spirit and guardian of the lake domain.

Cheverorm. Our equivalent of heaven, the place of reward in the afterlife.

Draenth. A mentally imbalanced individual.

Forgar. The spirit and guardian of the forest domain

Jool. Courage or bravery.

Momo. The same as a mother, a term used with affection.

Merol. The spirit and guardian of the desert domain.

Nalwarendirtur. The hunting grounds of the afterlife, whereby the hunters earn their admittance into Cheverorm.

Nicipi. A person who is weak or soft. Not strong.

Oquau. The regions of the deep waters, home of the Sisaryg.

Sisaryg. Underwater creatures, orange or red, with thick shells. Similar to our crabs or lobsters.

Soho. A young child, usually around 5 or 6 years of age.

www.ingramcontent.com/pod-product-compliance
Lightning Source LLC
Chambersburg PA
CBHW071224170626
46809CB00005BA/1926